A built-in best friend . . .

Jessica chose a pair of white plastic barrettes in the shape of bows from her dresser. "Let's wear these today. They go with our sweatsuits."

Elizabeth found her own matching barrettes. Then the twins stood in front of the mirror pinning their hair back. Because of the reflection in the mirror, there were now *four* identical girls instead of just two.

Elizabeth smiled at Jessica's reflection. She knew she and Jessica would always be best friends. That was what being twins was all about.

SWEET VALLEY KIDS

SURPRISE! SURPRISE!

Written by
Molly Mia Stewart

Created by
FRANCINE PASCAL

Illustrated by
Ying-Hwa Hu

A BANTAM SKYLARK BOOK®
NEW YORK · TORONTO · LONDON · SYDNEY · AUCKLAND

RL 2, 005-008

SURPRISE! SURPRISE!
A Bantam Skylark Book / November 1989

*Sweet Valley High® and Sweet Valley Kids are trademarks of
Francine Pascal.*

*Conceived by Francine Pascal
Produced by Daniel Weiss Associates, Inc.,
27 West 20th Street
New York, NY 10011*

Cover art by Susan Tang

*Skylark Books is a registered trademark of Bantam Books, a division of
Bantam Doubleday Dell Publishing Group, Inc.*

ISBN 0-553-15758-2

Published simultaneously in the United States and Canada

*Bantam Books are published by Bantam Books, a division of Bantam Double-
day Dell Publishing Group, Inc. Its trademark, consisting of the words
"Bantam Books" and the portrayal of a rooster, is Registered in U.S. Patent
and Trademark Office and in other countries. Marca Registrada. Bantam
Books, 666 Fifth Avenue, New York, New York 10103.*

PRINTED IN THE UNITED STATES OF AMERICA

O   0 9 8 7 6 5 4 3

To Molly Jessica W. Wenk

CHAPTER 1

Six Days to Go

Elizabeth Wakefield opened her eyes. She had a feeling that something good was about to happen.

Then she remembered. It was only six days until her seventh birthday.

"Jessica!" she called softly. "Wake up!" She threw her stuffed koala at the other bed in the room she shared with her twin sister. "Mmf-mumum," came a reply from under the covers. "Is it time to get up already?" asked a grumpy voice.

"Yes! Jess, only six days left!" Elizabeth

hopped out of her bed and stood beside Jessica's. "Isn't that great?"

Jessica sat up slowly and stretched like a kitten waking up from a nap. "Six days until what?" she asked. Then she opened her blue-green eyes wide. "Six days till our birthday! I almost forgot!"

Elizabeth and Jessica Wakefield were the only identical twins at Sweet Valley Elementary School. They looked exactly alike. They both had long blond hair, which they wore with bangs, and blue-green eyes. Whenever they smiled, a dimple appeared in their left cheeks.

Being twins was fun. They sat next to each other in Mrs. Becker's second-grade class. Elizabeth often knew what Jessica was going to say before Jessica said it, and sometimes

2

Jessica could tell what Elizabeth was thinking, too.

But even though they were twins and best friends, Jessica and Elizabeth didn't always like the same things. Jessica was noisy and Elizabeth was quiet. Jessica passed notes to her friends during class and was always ready to whisper with them. Elizabeth was an attentive student who read a lot. She also liked to write short poems. She could be by herself for hours.

"What are you wearing today?" Elizabeth asked.

"Let's both wear our yellow sweatsuits," Jessica said.

They had many matching outfits. Sometimes they chose the same thing in a different color. But not today!

"No one will be able to tell us apart," Elizabeth said. She reached into their closet and pulled out her yellow sweatsuit with tiny white flowers painted on it.

"Not unless they look at our wrists," Jessica replied. The twins had matching name bracelets that they wore to school every day.

Jessica was still looking for her yellow sweatsuit. Her side of the closet was much messier than Elizabeth's. Finally, Jessica found her sweatsuit on the floor in a corner of the closet.

"I wonder what we'll get for lunch today," Jessica said, pulling her sweatshirt over her head.

"I hope it's tuna fish," Elizabeth said. "And the peanut-butter cookies we had yesterday."

"Me, too," Jessica said.

Jessica chose a pair of white plastic barrettes in the shape of bows from her dresser. "Let's wear these today. They go with our sweatsuits."

Elizabeth found her own matching barrettes. Then the twins stood in front of the mirror pinning their hair back. Because of the reflection in the mirror, there were now *four* identical girls instead of just two.

Elizabeth smiled at Jessica's reflection. She knew she and Jessica would always be best friends. That was what being twins was all about.

CHAPTER 2

Twin Birthdays

Jessica hopped off the school bus and took Elizabeth's hand. The girls walked toward the entrance to Sweet Valley Elementary School.

"Do you think our spelling test will be hard?" Jessica asked.

"Don't worry," Elizabeth answered. "You'll do fine."

Jessica hoped that was true. Her sister always got better grades than she did. Jessica couldn't believe that Elizabeth actually liked doing homework. Luckily, Elizabeth always helped Jessica with her assignments. Sometimes Elizabeth even did her arithmetic problems for her.

A group of second-grade girls was already standing outside Mrs. Becker's room when the twins got there.

"Jessica! Elizabeth! Hi!" A girl named Lila Fowler ran toward them.

Lila had on a brand-new pair of sneakers. She wore something new almost every day. Jessica wished she could have as many clothes as Lila. After Elizabeth, Lila was Jessica's favorite friend.

Elizabeth didn't like Lila as much as Jessica did. Sometimes Lila was bossy and acted like she was better than everyone else. She almost never let anyone borrow pencils from her, even though she always had extras.

"I have to ask Mrs. Becker something," Elizabeth said, and walked into the classroom.

Jessica stayed outside with Lila. Another girl, named Ellen Riteman, came over and stood with them. Lois Waller looked like she wanted to join them, but Lila stared at her in a mean way until she went inside. Lois was chubby and Lila loved to tease her.

"I can't *wait* for your party," Lila told Jessica excitedly.

"Me, neither," Ellen chimed in.

"Neither can I!" Jessica said. It was only Monday. The party was planned for Saturday. Jessica and Elizabeth needed the whole week to plan the details.

Lila stuck her nose in the air. "I got you a

really good present," she told Jessica in an "I know something you don't know" voice.

"What is it? Tell me!" Jessica hopped up and down with excitement. She grabbed Lila's hand. "Please, please, *please* tell me," she begged.

"No. It's a surprise."

Jessica wished she knew a secret she could trade with Lila. She didn't think she could wait until Saturday to find out what her present was.

"Give me a hint."

Lila crossed her arms and shook her head. "N-O means no. If I told you, then it wouldn't be a secret anymore."

Jessica looked hopefully at Ellen. "Do you know what she's getting me?"

"Don't tell!" Lila said to Ellen in a bossy voice. She folded her arms.

"Please? Pretty please?" Jessica gave Lila a pleading look.

"Well," Lila said slowly. She loved to act mysterious. "It's something good."

Jessica wrinkled her nose. "Is it something I want?"

Lila nodded with a big smile on her face. Ellen giggled.

Jessica wondered what it could be. She had a two-page birthday list of everything she wanted, including a pony and a guitar like Lila's. She hoped she would get everything on the list.

"What did you get for Elizabeth?" Lila asked.

"Elizabeth?" Jessica clapped one hand over her mouth.

Ellen tilted her head to one side. "It's her birthday, too, remember?"

Jessica gulped. "I know, but I forgot." Her cheeks turned pink.

She looked in through the classroom door. Her sister was talking to a thin boy named Winston Egbert. He was always trying to make people laugh with his clown faces. Plus, he ate peanut butter and *mayonnaise* sandwiches. Jessica didn't know how Elizabeth could talk to him.

She also didn't know how she could forget her own sister's birthday. She felt terrible.

"OK, class," called out Mrs. Becker, their teacher. "Settle down!"

Jessica, Lila, and Ellen went inside and

took their seats. Everyone else was running to sit down, too. Andy Franklin knocked his books off his desk. When he bent over to pick them up, his glasses fell off. Jessica laughed.

Mrs. Becker began to review last night's homework.

Jessica rested her chin on her left hand as the class answered Mrs. Becker's questions. Elizabeth seemed to know every answer, but all Jessica could think about was Elizabeth. She had to get her the best present ever.

She knew exactly what *she* wanted for her birthday. She could get the same thing for Elizabeth.

". . . That's very good, class." Mrs. Becker said, as she began to pass out the spelling tests.

Jessica looked over at her twin sister and smiled.

I know the perfect birthday present for Elizabeth, she thought.

CHAPTER 3

Party Plans

Elizabeth and Jessica walked to the bus stop on Tuesday morning with their brother, Steven, who was in fifth grade.

"Are you excited yet about our party?" Elizabeth asked.

"Yes!" Jessica answered. "It's going to be so much fun."

Steven made a face. "Who wants to go to a dumb girls' party?" he said. He ran ahead. Steven usually pretended he didn't know

Elizabeth and Jessica. And when he didn't ignore the twins, he teased them.

"It won't be dumb," Elizabeth shouted to Steven. She was walking carefully, pretending the sidewalk was a tightrope. "Right, Jessica?" she asked.

Jessica nodded. "Right. Everyone in the whole class is invited. It's going to be really, really, really good. And we'll get tons of presents."

"What food should we have?" Elizabeth asked. It was an important question. The girls thought as they walked.

"I know!" Elizabeth said. "How about hot dogs and hamburgers. We can have a cookout!"

Jessica shook her head. "That's too messy,"

18

she complained. "I always get catsup on my hands and the bun always falls apart."

"So what?" Elizabeth teased. "I don't care."

Jessica shook her head again. "No way."

"Then how about Mexican tacos?" Elizabeth suggested. "Those are fun, because you get to put in anything you like."

"Yuck!" Jessica shook her head. "They always break."

Elizabeth stuck her hands in her blue-jeans pockets. "OK, then what do *you* want?" she said.

They stopped to wait for the school bus along with lots of other kids. Their classmate Todd Wilkins was joking around with his friends. When he saw the twins he came over and pretended to punch Elizabeth.

Elizabeth jumped aside. "Quit it," she said, giggling. Todd always chased her during recess, but she could run faster.

"Let's have corn on the cob," Jessica said. She raised her arms over her head in a dance pose.

"We can't," Elizabeth said as she pointed to her loose tooth. "Remember?" It was going to fall out any day.

"Oh, I forgot." Jessica giggled. She touched her own loose tooth.

"You could have pudding," Todd said. "You can eat it with straws."

Jessica stuck her tongue out at him. He laughed and ran over to Charlie Cashman, who was in their class, too.

Jessica struck another dance pose. The twins went to modern dance class after school on Tuesdays. Jessica only began to practice on Tuesday mornings.

"Grilled cheese sandwiches aren't as messy as hamburgers," Jessica told Elizabeth. "Wouldn't that be good?"

Elizabeth thought it over carefully. She wanted to think of the best party food. It had to be something that everyone liked. And it had to be special. Maybe hamburgers and grilled cheese sandwiches weren't special enough. They could have those any day in the school cafeteria.

She looked at the other kids waiting for the bus. Charlie was teasing a first grader. "Sausage-head," Charlie shouted. He made a monster face and ran off with one of the boy's books.

Elizabeth looked at Jessica. "How about

tiny pizzas?" she asked. They both liked pizza a lot.

Jessica's eyes sparkled. "Neat! I love pizza!"

"We can get lots of different kinds," Elizabeth said. "Sausage, mushroom—"

"Extra cheese," Jessica interrupted excitedly. "And those little salamis."

"They're called pepperonis," Elizabeth told her twin. "I was just going to say that!"

They looked at each other and laughed. It was fun to think alike.

Now they knew exactly what to serve for their birthday party. It was going to be their best birthday ever!

CHAPTER 4

Jessica's Secret Plan

Jessica stood in front of the wall-sized mirror at modern dance class. She was wearing a black leotard with pink tights. She could see the whole class in the mirror. Lila came in wearing a new red leotard and red leg warmers. Lila had more leotards than anyone.

"Will you help me do my ponytail over?" Elizabeth asked. She skipped over to Jessica.

Jessica took Elizabeth's ponytail holder and fixed her sister's hair.

"Thanks," Elizabeth said.

Jessica checked her own ponytail in the mirror. She smiled when she saw it was perfect.

Ms. Garber, their dance teacher, entered the studio. She had long red hair in a braid that came all the way down her back. She clapped her hands twice. "Everyone to your places, please!"

Jessica lined up behind Elizabeth. Lila stood to her right. The whole class began the warm-up exercises.

"And down and up and down and up! Bend your knees!" Ms. Garber put a tape in the tape deck. "We're going to try a new step today."

"But I still don't know the last one!" Lois

wailed. She was going down when everyone else was going up.

"Everyone's talking about your party," Lila whispered to Jessica.

Jessica grinned at Lila. "I can't wait. We invited everyone in the whole class."

"Even Winston Egbert?" Lila said. She giggled. "He'll eat your whole cake!"

Jessica giggled, too. Winston ate more than anyone else she knew, even Steven.

"Ellen told me what she's getting you," Lila whispered.

Ms. Garber clapped her hands again. "Quiet, girls! Concentrate, please! And be graceful."

Jessica made sure Ms. Garber was looking the other way before she looked over at Lila

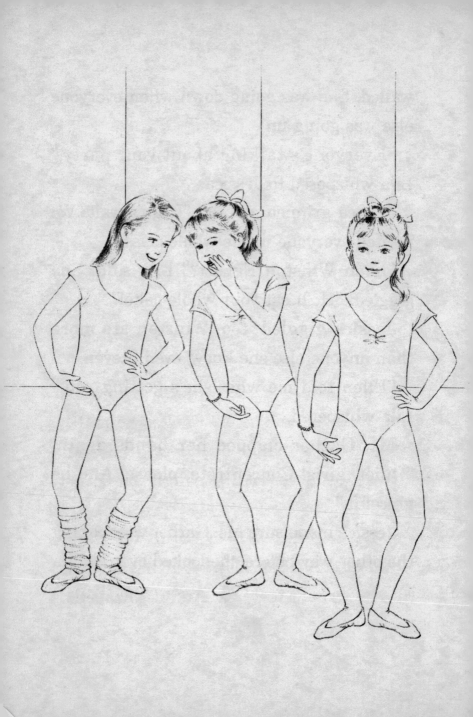

again. "What's Ellen getting me?" she whispered back as she did her knee bends.

Lila went down and up and down and up. She shook her head. "I can't tell you."

Jessica stuck her tongue out at Lila. Then she faced front again.

"Are you getting a new dress for your party?" Lila asked.

Jessica nodded without turning her head. "Me, too. So is Ellen."

Jessica thought about Elizabeth's present again. The last time she went to the mall, she had seen a light blue velvet headband with a bow on it. Jessica thought it was beautiful.

Jessica couldn't wait to buy it for Elizabeth. But that would be tricky. They always went everywhere together. And if Elizabeth went with Jessica to buy the bow, the present wouldn't be a surprise. Just this once, Jessica decided, she would have to do something separately from her twin.

CHAPTER 5

The Perfect Present

It was Wednesday. Elizabeth was reading *Hedgehog Holiday* and eating cinnamon raisin toast for breakfast. It was her favorite kind of toast. It was Jessica's favorite, too.

Jessica wasn't at the breakfast table, though. Neither was Mrs. Wakefield.

"Where's Mom?" Steven asked. He sat down at the table and started gulping his orange juice.

Mr. Wakefield was reading the newspaper. "She and Jess had something to talk about."

Elizabeth was surprised. Jessica never had private talks without her. She bit around the edge of her toast until there was no crust left. She didn't feel like reading anymore.

Jessica and Mrs. Wakefield finally came into the kitchen.

Elizabeth looked at her sister. Jessica was smiling.

"Elizabeth, would you like to play at Caroline's house after school?" their mother asked.

"Sure," Elizabeth said. Caroline Pearce was in their class. She lived two houses away from the Wakefields. "Do you want to, Jessica?"

Jessica took a bite of her toast and a sip of milk. She didn't say anything.

"Jessica and I have a few errands to do

after school," Mrs. Wakefield replied. "We'll be back at four-thirty."

Elizabeth's eyes widened. "Where are you going?" she asked her twin sister.

"It's a secret," Jessica answered. She bit a big piece from her toast.

Elizabeth couldn't figure out what the secret was. She wondered all the way to school. But Jessica wouldn't tell.

In the afternoon, the class arranged leaves on paper. Elizabeth squished some glue around with her finger. She tried to make a nice design, but all she could think about was Jessica's secret.

Ellen was sitting next to Jessica, across the table from Elizabeth. Jessica was whispering something in Ellen's ear. Ellen was smiling. Then they both laughed.

Elizabeth felt angry. "What's so funny?" she asked.

"Nothing," Jessica said. She giggled again and pressed down one of her leaves.

Elizabeth looked at her design. She felt sad. Jessica always told her everything. Why was she keeping a secret from her now?

"Don't pay any attention to them," Amy Sutton whispered to Elizabeth. Amy was Elizabeth's best friend after Jessica.

"I know," Elizabeth said. She was still wondering, though.

"Hey!" Lois yelped suddenly. Everyone looked at her. She was twisting her neck and trying to see the back of her shirt. Charlie Cashman ran across the room with a grin on his face.

"He glued a leaf to you," Caroline said.

33

"Mrs. Becker! Charlie glued a leaf on Lois!"

"Now, now, quiet down." Mrs. Becker unglued the leaf from Lois's back and brought it over to Charlie.

Elizabeth's fingers were getting all sticky, so she rubbed off the glue and rolled it into a little ball. She flicked it onto Jessica's paper. She hoped it would make Jessica tell her secret.

"I'm still not going to tell you," Jessica said.

Jessica always knew just what Elizabeth was thinking.

"OK," Elizabeth said grumpily.

She hoped Jessica would tell her later. They had never had secrets from each other before.

CHAPTER 6

The Secret Mission

Jessica could think only of the birthday party. When Mrs. Becker asked them to spell chocolate, Jessica thought about chocolate cake.

Mrs. Wakefield was going to order a special chocolate cake with marshmallow icing and sprinkles on top. "Maybe I should get two cakes," she had said. "Twin cakes for my twin girls." Just thinking about it made Jessica excited.

"Pssst," someone whispered.

Jessica turned around. Todd Wilkins sat behind her. He was leaning forward.

"What do you want?" she said softly.

"Do you want robots or garbage goo for a present?" he asked.

Jessica made a face. Garbage goo was slimy and came in a miniature garbage can.

"Only boys like that stuff," Jessica said. "It's gross. And I don't like robots, either."

Elizabeth looked over at her sister and shook her head. Jessica often got into trouble for whispering in class.

Todd shot a little wad of paper over to Elizabeth's desk. She looked down, but she was smiling.

"Just get me something pretty," Jessica said firmly.

Todd pretended to gag.

"Jessica!" Mrs. Becker said. "No talking, please."

Caroline turned around and said "Shh!" very loudly, just the way Mrs. Becker did.

Jessica ignored her. She tore a piece of paper out of her notebook. "NO YUCKY STUFF!" she wrote in big dark capitals. She folded the paper up and placed it on Todd's desk.

"Do you like stuffed animals?" Ken Matthews asked in a whisper. He sat next to Todd. "My little cousin has a stuffed tiger she doesn't like. I could give it to you."

Jessica shook her head. "I don't want a little kid's present," she said. She looked at Elizabeth. "Boys always think of such dumb presents."

Ken moved his chair closer. "How about a catcher's mitt?"

"Sure!" Elizabeth said. Then her cheeks turned pink and she clamped one hand over her mouth.

"No way!" Jessica whispered. But she liked having lots of people pay attention to her.

Waiting for birthday presents was almost as much fun as the party itself!

After school, Jessica left for the mall with her mother.

"I hope you didn't tell Lizzie where we're going, Mom," she said.

Mrs. Wakefield shook her head. "I didn't, honey. I promised you this morning."

"And don't tell her what I'm getting her," Jessica said. She gave her mother a serious look. "It's a secret. Don't give it away."

Her mother crossed her heart and snapped her fingers twice. That was their secret promise signal. "I won't."

"Good." Jessica bounced on the seat of the car. She couldn't wait to get Elizabeth's present.

"Have you given this present a lot of thought?" Mrs. Wakefield asked.

Jessica stopped bouncing. "Sure, Mom. It's the only thing I've been thinking about for two days!"

When they got to the store, there were many pretty bows and barrettes to choose from. Jessica liked them all, and had a hard time choosing between the blue velvet bow, and a beautiful pink silky one. She tried them on her own hair.

"I think I'll get Liz the velvet bow," Jessica decided as she admired herself in the counter mirror.

Mrs. Wakefield's eyebrows went up in an arch. "Are you absolutely positive that's the kind of thing Elizabeth would want?" she asked.

Jessica nodded quickly. "Absolutely positive! She'll love it. It's what I want someone to give me."

"OK," her mother said. "When we get home, we'll wrap it up together and make it look just right."

Jessica couldn't contain her excitement. "Only three days left!" she said. "I can't wait to surprise her!"

CHAPTER 7

Elizabeth's Secret Plan

On Thursday, Elizabeth, Jessica, and Steven raced to the kitchen when they got home from school.

"Whoa! What's the hurry?" Mrs. Wakefield asked.

"We're starving," Elizabeth said.

Elizabeth took a plate of creme sandwich cookies off the counter. She twisted one open and gave half to Jessica. Steven poured a glass of milk and drank it in three quick gulps. Elizabeth could hear the glug-glug-glug from his throat.

"Who knows what day it is?" their mother asked.

"Thursday," Jessica told her. She scraped the creme off her cookie with her bottom teeth.

Mrs. Wakefield looked pleased. "Thursday? Thursday is party-dress shopping day."

"Hooray!" Elizabeth and Jessica both shouted.

"We want the kind with a ruffle on the bottom and a big bow sash," Jessica said. She looked at Elizabeth. "Right?"

Elizabeth shook her head. "Not *really* frilly or we'll look like dolls."

"Party dresses," Steven said, grabbing his

throat with both hands. Then he crossed his eyes and fell off his chair.

Elizabeth laughed. "You're such a clown, Steven."

As Elizabeth ate another half of a cookie, she smiled to herself. She was thinking about the present she had picked out for Jessica. It was a little race car that flipped over and spun in circles when it was wound up. Elizabeth thought it was really fun. She couldn't wait to see Jessica's expression when she unwrapped it.

Mrs. Wakefield hadn't seemed sure that Jessica would like getting a car, but Elizabeth was certain her twin would. "She'll love it as much as I do," Elizabeth had said.

Elizabeth had already given Mrs.

Wakefield the money to buy it. "Don't tell Jessica what it is. It's her birthday surprise."

"When you're ready, we'll go shopping," Mrs. Wakefield said.

"We're ready now," Elizabeth said, quickly twisting open her third cookie and popping half in her mouth at once.

Jessica was ready, too. "I can't wait! I love buying new clothes!" she said.

Elizabeth laughed. She still wondered what Jessica's secret was. But she was too excited about her own surprise to think about it too much.

The twins' favorite store in the mall was full of party clothes, school clothes, and play clothes. Elizabeth ran over to a green dress with short sleeves. "This is nice!" she said. "It doesn't look like a baby-doll dress."

"I like this one," Jessica said, holding up a pink dress with a puffy skirt and white lace.

Elizabeth made a face. She didn't like the pink one at all.

"That green one is no good, Liz," Jessica said. "It's just a school dress."

"But we couldn't play any games outside in the dress you like," Elizabeth explained. "It's too fancy."

Jessica pouted. "We don't *have* to play outside. We can play indoor games."

Mrs. Wakefield was looking at another rack. "Look around some more," she suggested. "We're not in a hurry."

Elizabeth and Jessica walked down another aisle.

"Do you like this one?" Jessica asked. She pointed to a black velvet dress with a red satin sash. Elizabeth crossed her eyes and continued to look.

Then, at the same time, they both grabbed the exact same dress.

"This one!" they both yelled. Their mother came over to look.

"But it doesn't have a ruffle or a bow," Mrs. Wakefield pointed out to Jessica.

"But I love it!" Jessica told her.

Mrs. Wakefield looked at Elizabeth. "And it's pretty dressy."

"But I love it, too!" Elizabeth said.

The dress was red with long sleeves, and it had small pink and green flowers on it.

Jessica held it up to herself. "Isn't it *beautiful?*"

Mrs. Wakefield held up another one against Elizabeth. "I think it's perfect. You'll be the stars of your party."

Jessica and Elizabeth both twirled around.

"And we'll get shiny new shoes to match," added Mrs. Wakefield. "You'll both sparkle from head to toe."

CHAPTER 8

Counting the Hours

At last it was Friday. In gym class, Mr. Butler announced they would run a three-legged race.

"I'll be your partner," Lila said to Jessica.

Julie Porter smiled at Elizabeth. "Will you be my partner?"

Other girls asked them, too. Jessica liked being popular. The twins shook their heads.

"Elizabeth is always my partner," Jessica said.

Elizabeth nodded. "Twins always stick to-gether."

Jessica knew they could run in a three-leg-ged race better than anyone else. And she knew they could win. Jessica and Elizabeth always ran in step. They were the perfect team.

Mr. Butler blew his whistle.

Jessica and Elizabeth got off to a fast start. Charlie Cashman and Jerry McAllister tripped Andy Franklin and Winston Egbert but got tangled up on their next step and fell behind.

Todd and Ken were running together. They were catching up to Jessica and Eliz-abeth. Then they fell down.

"We're going to win!" Elizabeth said.

They were ahead of everybody. Other pairs

were falling all around them. Lila and Ellen were still running, but they couldn't catch up.

Jessica and Elizabeth crossed the finish line first. They jumped up and down and gave each other a big hug. "We won!" Jessica laughed.

When they all got back to Mrs. Becker's room, some of the kids went to look at the class hamster. Her name was Tinkerbell. They were all taking turns bringing her home on the weekends.

"I hope we get a turn pretty soon," Elizabeth said.

Jessica shivered. "I don't want to! Tinkerbell's a rat!"

"No, she's not," Elizabeth replied. "I like her!"

Mrs. Becker asked everyone to sit down. "I know something special is happening tomorrow," she said. She looked at Jessica and Elizabeth. "So I brought in brownies for everyone. It's an early celebration for Elizabeth and Jessica."

Mrs. Becker brought brownies to class each time it was someone's birthday. She was a nice teacher.

Two of the brownies had candles stuck in them. Mrs. Becker carefully lit a match. The candles started to glow.

"Happy Birthday one day early," Mrs. Becker sang. The rest of the class joined in. Winston sang the loudest.

Caroline raised her hand. "Can I help pass the brownies out?" she asked. She was always eager to help the teacher.

Mrs. Becker smiled. "Thank you, Caroline." The teacher handed the brownies with candles to Jessica and Elizabeth while Caroline passed brownies to everyone else.

"Only one day to B-day, you guys," Winston said. He stuffed a whole brownie in his mouth and chewed. When he smiled there was chocolate between his teeth.

"Gross, Winston!" Jessica cried.

Winston turned around so everyone could see. Todd and Ken showed their own dark teeth.

Jessica shook her head and laughed. She was so excited she was starting to count the hours!

CHAPTER 9

Party Time

"Jessica! Wake up!" Elizabeth said as she bounced on her sister's bed. "It's our birthday!"

Jessica sat up. Today she smiled instead of growling like she usually did.

"Good morning, birthday girls!" Mr. Wakefield walked in and gave both girls big hugs. "How does it feel to be seven?"

"Great, Daddy," Elizabeth replied happily.

Jessica nodded. "So far, it's better than being six."

"Terrific! Hurry up, now. Your mother's making a special birthday breakfast for you," Mr. Wakefield said. "And then we'll put the finishing touch on your decorations."

After their breakfast of blueberry pancakes with maple syrup, the twins put up pink, white, and yellow streamers. Mr. Wakefield blew up matching balloons. He pretended it was hard work. Each time he took a breath, his eyes got wide and his cheeks puffed out.

"Time to put on your new party dresses," Mrs. Wakefield said when they were done.

"Try to sit still so I can brush your hair," she told Elizabeth.

"I can't!" Elizabeth giggled. "I feel like I have ants in my pants!"

Jessica was spinning around in front of the mirror.

"Your new dresses look beautiful, girls," Mrs. Wakefield said. "It's a very special day."

Elizabeth and Jessica picked out matching barrettes. Then they were ready!

Winston was the first person to arrive at the party. He held out a big, lumpy-looking present. The wrapping paper was wrinkled and the bow was not quite tied.

"I wrapped it myself," he said proudly. His hair was combed down with water, but one piece stuck up in back.

Soon all the others arrived. A large pile of colorful presents was stacked on the living room table.

"When are you going to open them?" Lois asked.

"After we play some games," Elizabeth explained. She looked at her twin sister. She was having so much fun!

The Wakefield house was as noisy as the school lunchroom. Some of the boys were making airplane sounds and chasing each other around.

Mrs. Wakefield blew on a party horn. "OK, kids! It's time to play our first game."

"Pin the tail on the donkey?" Jessica asked.

"Nope." Mrs. Wakefield laughed. "Sardines!"

Elizabeth screamed. "My favorite!" She grabbed Jessica's hand. "Do we get to hide first?"

"Elizabeth and Jessica will hide while everyone else covers their eyes," their mother said. "Everyone count up to twenty and then start looking. When you find Elizabeth and Jessica, you hide with them. The last person to find them has to hide next time. Ready?

"One, two, three . . ."

Elizabeth and Jessica ran out of the living room.

"Let's get in the bathtub in Mom and Dad's bathroom," Elizabeth whispered. "That's the best hiding place."

Jessica giggled. They tiptoed upstairs. After they climbed in the bathtub, they pulled the curtain across.

Elizabeth held her breath. She could hear their friends looking for them.

Jessica giggled again but quickly covered her mouth with her hands.

They heard footsteps. Todd peeked behind the curtain.

"Shhh!" Elizabeth whispered. "Climb in quickly."

Next, Amy found them. "Come on," Jessica said, pulling Amy in.

Soon the bathtub was crowded. Everyone was giggling and whispering "Shh!"

"Who hasn't found us yet?" Jessica asked.

At the same time, three people whispered, "Winston."

"Here I am!" Winston yelled. He yanked the curtain back.

Everyone screamed and stepped out of the tub.

"Come on down!" Mr. Wakefield called. "Time to open the presents!"

CHAPTER 10

The Big Surprise

"Open mine first!" Lila said.

Ellen jumped up and down. "No! Mine!"

Jessica looked at the big pile. There were so many presents. She wanted to open them all at once!

"Which one should we open first?" she asked her sister.

Elizabeth's cheeks were pink with excitement. "I don't know! I can't decide."

"How about opening the presents in the

order that your friends arrived?" their mother suggested.

"Me! I was first!" Winston shouted. He jumped up and grabbed his gift.

Jessica and Elizabeth took it and sat down. The present felt soft and squishy. Together they ripped off the paper.

Two stuffed dinosaurs fell out.

"Hey!" Jessica said. She picked one up and hugged it. "These are nice!"

Elizabeth hugged hers, too. "Thanks, Win."

"I was next," Lila said.

She held out two large boxes. Jessica's had a silver bow and Elizabeth's had a gold bow.

"What is it?" Jessica gasped. She shook her box and heard a rattling sound.

"Open it and see!" Lila told her.

They undid the paper at the same time. Jessica took one look and screamed.

"A dollhouse! This is the best!"

She hugged Lila. The dollhouse needed to be assembled, but the picture on the box was very pretty.

"And I got furniture for the dollhouse!" Elizabeth said. "Little miniature chairs and tables! Aren't they neat?"

"I knew you'd get us something really good, Lila," Jessica said.

"Open mine next," Todd said. "I got something different for each of you because you're both different."

Elizabeth and Jessica opened their presents from Todd at the same time. Jessica's was a necklace with a ballerina charm, and

Elizabeth's was a shiny notebook with a picture of a cute hamster on it.

"Thanks, Todd," Jessica said, putting her necklace on.

Elizabeth smiled. "This is a really good notebook. The hamster looks just like Tinkerbell."

It took a long time to open all the presents. Jessica and Elizabeth were surrounded by wrapping paper and ribbons and pieces of tape. Amy gave Elizabeth two new books, and Jessica an autograph album. Ellen gave each twin leg warmers for dance class, and Ken gave them a poster of a rainbow for their bedroom.

Finally, there were only two presents left.

"This is what I got you," Jessica told Elizabeth.

Elizabeth held out a little box with a bow. "And this is what I got you," Elizabeth said.

Jessica took a deep breath. "Let's open them at the same time," she said. "OK?"

"OK."

Everyone was quiet. Jessica and Elizabeth tore off the paper. "Gee, Liz," Jessica said without enthusiasm. "This is . . . nice." Elizabeth was equally surprised by her present.

"Oh," she said, holding the blue velvet bow and looking puzzled. "Ummm . . . thanks, Jess."

Todd spoke up. "Maybe you got the boxes mixed up."

Lila and Ellen giggled. Jessica kept looking at the car, looking at the headband, and looking back again.

"Aren't you going to say anything?" Lila said loudly.

Jessica and Elizabeth looked at each other. Then, at the exact same instant, they held out the presents and switched. Everyone laughed.

"I got you what I wanted," Elizabeth admitted.

"And I got you what I wanted," Jessica said, shaking her head. Everyone laughed again.

Elizabeth started winding up her car. "Next year, I'll pick something *you* would like."

"Me, too," Jessica said, putting on her headband. "I bought this for you on Wednesday," she added.

Elizabeth gasped. "Was that the secret?"

"Yup!"

"Now I know," Elizabeth said. She looked happy.

"Time for birthday cake!" Mrs. Wakefield announced.

They all ran into the dining room. Mr. Wakefield turned off the lights and went into the kitchen.

Everyone was quiet. Jessica and Elizabeth held hands.

Then their mother and father came back in. They were each carrying a birthday cake that had marshmallow icing with beautiful flowers around the edges. And both cakes had lots of chocolate sprinkles on top.

"Happy Birthday to You!" Mr. and Mrs. Wakefield sang.

Everyone joined in.

Jessica and Elizabeth each blew out the eight pink candles on their cakes. There was an extra one for good luck.

"Don't forget to make a wish," Amy said.

Jessica smiled at Elizabeth. "Being twins is the best thing in the world."

Elizabeth giggled. "That goes double for me." She picked up the notebook from Todd and hugged it. She hoped her birthday wish would come true. There was nothing she wanted more than to bring Tinkerbell home over the winter vacation.

What will Jessica do if Elizabeth brings the class hamster home? Find out in Sweet Valley Kids #2, RUNAWAY HAMSTER.

SWEET VALLEY KIDS

Jessica and Elizabeth have had lots of adventures in *Sweet Valley High* and *Sweet Valley Twins*...now read about the twins at age seven! You'll love all the fun that comes with being seven—birthday parties, playing dress-up, class projects, putting on puppet shows and plays, losing a tooth, setting up lemonade stands, caring for animals and much more! It's all part of SWEET VALLEY KIDS. Read them all!